# ALL I WANT IS A KISS

WILLOW WINTERS

## OLIVIA

The butterflies in my stomach just won't quit it. I've searched the lobby with baited breath, but he's not here. Nick's all I could think about the entire flight. I was so convinced I'd step in through those double glass doors behind me and see him standing right in front of me, not this thin crowd of people I don't recognize.

The entire flight I pictured him at the end of the mahogany bar, seated on the leather stool with his gray tailored suit. He knows the one I like; it brings out his steely eyes. They're such a pale blue, I swear sometimes they're silver. At least they look that way under the dimmed bar lights late at night in this very hotel.

I imagined coming up beside him at the bar, and

casually ordering a drink, pretending not to recognize him. As if I wouldn't know his cologne, his confident, dominating demeanor, that rough stubbled jaw in a heartbeat. I swear my body can recognize his in a crowd a mile away. I'm simply drawn to him. I even changed into this red dress that clings to my curves at the airport and touched up my makeup, just for that moment. Last time I saw him, he told me I look gorgeous in red. Pouty red lips. Check. Sultry red dress. Check check. Man I've been dreaming about for days? Nowhere in sight.

Sighing, I roll out my shoulder, letting my luggage bag fall to the crook of my arm for only a moment. It gives me enough time to take in the place without thoughts of *him* making me an anxious, excited mess. The gust of cold from behind me urges me forward, away from the front entrance and back to reality.

It's bitter cold in the Pennsylvania mountains and I happen to despise the cold. We aren't friends. No way, no how. But the fireplaces in the ski lodge resort this hotel is based in, made of large stones and surrounded by plush leather couches? We may as well be old lovers.

"There you are!" Over the din of chatter from the

crowded bar across the lobby. I recognize Autumn's voice instantly.

"Hey, hey love," I greet her with a peppy voice and a tight hug when we meet halfway. Her embrace is only half assed, but she's got a good reason. Standing two inches shorter than me with big brown eyes and a brunette bob, Autumn has a wine glass in each of her hands. Red for her, and white for me. The red in her glass matches her soft chenille sweater perfectly too. As if she did it on purpose.

"I freaking love you," I say gratefully, tossing down the weekender duffle and graciously accepting the glass. If I can't have him, my heart flips in protest at the thought, at least I can have a little wine to take the edge off.

"I'm telling you," my friend of over a decade is always "telling me" something. She's also typically right. Maybe always right, I'm not sure, I don't have the mental energy to keep track. She's the creative one, I'm the workaholic. Together we kick ass. "It's so much better when you come a day early."

"I seriously wish I could, but--"

"Work," she finishes the sentence for me and rolls her eyes when she does. "I know," she comments before sipping her red wine. Her bottom lip is

3

already slightly stained, but it only adds to her charm.

"You would think with the way you said 'work' that you don't know we're actually here for work." With my glass in my left hand and my luggage in my right, I make my way to the elevators.

"A conference is different and you know it." Autumn follows behind me, offering to take my glass. With a smirk I tell her she'll have to kill me to get it from me. It's chilled and delicious and exactly what I need after a long flight. I thought I would be here hours ago, but the flight was delayed, and here I am arriving at eleven at night with tired, dry eyes. A glass of wine is exactly what I need.

"Fine, give me your bag," she insists, downing the rest of her red. I want to ask her if she's seen Nick, but I don't. I keep my lips sealed tight, grateful that she's at least here to greet me. Besides, I know she knows I'm looking for him. I always am at these events. If she saw him, she'd tell me. The simper on my face wavers slightly, but only slightly.

A lobby attendant passes by and collects the now empty wine glass from her just as the door to the spacious elevator opens. "Thank you," she offers the uniformed gentleman. Maybe it's the uniform, or maybe I'm just really in need, but the guy is *hot*. Like he came out of a People's sexiest men alive list, *hot*. His smile is charming, a little too wide and Autumn actually blushes before pushing me into the elevator.

"You aren't kidding," I tell her as the doors close and I take another sip, "I really should have gotten in last night." The smile that creeps onto my face is fitting for the Cheshire cat.

Autumn only laughs. She's all sorts of good bundled into a beautiful little package. "Oh fuck off," she jokes back. "I wish I had the balls for a one-night stand."

There's a little blip in my chest, and heat rolls down my shoulders, yet it gives my arms chills at the thought. I was hoping for a one night stand with a man I've had plenty of those with. Disappointment lingers, he knows I'm here for the conference and every time I come to the East Coast, we meet up. Every single time. One to two times a month for nearly two years now. He's not my boyfriend; and I don't want him to be. We want different things in life and we live on opposite sides of the country. There's an unspoken commitment though. I'm the only one he sees, and he's the only one I see. It's casual and low maintenance. But why does it feel so crushing that I haven't heard from him yet?

I text him yesterday and he said he'd be here.

5

He's just not here yet. That's what it is. I try to convince myself and then resort to sticking my nose into Autumn's business to take my mind off of it.

"I mean...," I tease her, "we are staying for an entire weekend. And since you came a day early, it could be a four-day-stand."

I can tell she must be at least half a bottle in by how loud she laughs and it only makes me want to catch up as we make our way to the room. I have an order to things though, before I can have more than this one glass. I don't just drop off my luggage in the room like Autumn does, I unpack everything. I put it in its place. I get bottles of water and my ear plugs and put them on the night stand too. I'm just a little OCD like that. It helps me feel settled.

"This one's for you," she hands over a keycard without acknowledging my comment, simply shaking her head in feigned dismay.

This is the same lodge as last year and it doesn't escape my knowledge when we get off the elevator that this is the same floor Nick was on last year. I spent an extra two days with him last time, lost in the sheets and taking off from work for the first time in months just to prolong saying goodbye.

I have to blow a stray piece of blonde out of my

face and focus. This trip is not about him, no matter how much my libido may disagree.

Autumn's already plopped herself onto a bed. She knows the drill.

At first, when we started going to all of these events so frequently, she would stare at me like I was an alien with two heads whenever we bunked for a conference, but now, she lays back on her bed, kicks her feet up and gives me the itinerary while I do my thing. All the while, her bag lays on the floor, unzipped and spilling out everything she packed. Except her dresses, which are always hung up in the closet. She gets the right side, which she barely uses, and I get the left.

"I'm glad you're finally here. I was thinking I wasn't going to make it and by the time you got here I'd be dead asleep."

"I should have just gotten on the flight with you."

"Yes," she says pointedly as I unzip my bag. "Yes you should have." The way she says it makes me laugh. She is *always right* after all and her tone doesn't hide that fact.

"Hey," I finally get the courage to ask her although I turn my back to her, busying myself with my clothes, "did you happen to hear from Nick?"

"Mmm. Not yet." She answers and I let the frown

stay in place as I put everything away. "Am I already boring you?" she asks with humor dripping on every word.

I turn to look over my shoulder, folding a pair of jeans to slip in the dresser drawer, "You know I love you."

We may be completely opposite in a lot of ways, but we're also a perfect match. Autumn and I started this marketing meet up company together and when we did I questioned if we really should. I didn't want to risk a decade long friendship over business. I'm so glad we took the risk though. Three years later and we're closer than ever and the business practically runs itself. We connect businesses with the firms they need to take their companies to the next level. I evaluate them, every nook and cranny and data point they have to offer to identify what they're lacking and how they can improve. Autumn does the socializing and connecting and most importantly, updating our clients and keeping them on track.

"So it kicks off tomorrow with a key note speech at noon, lunch served during. Then we have a workshop with the promotional team."

"You sound bored as all hell," I call out as I make my way to the bathroom to put my toiletries in their place. We've been through these conferences a dozen times this winter already. All the clients are new, but the talks are the same. So "bored" is a word that's rather accurate to describe how we'd feel if we had to sit in on the talks. This is the last one before the holidays then we have a decent break. I'm looking forward to PJs and downtime.

Autumn gets stuck attending the workshops this time around. Luckily, I'll be meeting with every client one on one, face to face, making sure we're on the same page and they're comfortable with the conclusion we've come to. Change can be unwanted, and even scary at times. But, like I tell each and every one of them, change is necessary. If you want to be at a level you've never been to before, you need to do something you've never done before.

"I don't come here for the lectures." Autumn stretches on the bed and adds with a yawn, "You don't either."

"Let me guess, is it for the lobby attendees and booze?"

She belts out a laugh and corrects me, "Again, I freaking wish." I'm still busy unpacking when she comments, "Speaking of getting some—"

"You're getting some?" Both of us have been single for nearly two years. My reason is easy; I'm only interested in what I have with Nick at the moment. I don't see a reason to stop or to want more. Although that's not something I shout from the rooftops.

Instead, I stick with something simple for an excuse as to why there's no ring on my finger: I'm a workaholic and my expectations are unreasonable. At least that's what my therapist said. And by therapist, I mean a bottle of Cabernet and a slurring best friend by the name of Autumn. Even though she's well aware of the truth, after all, Nick is her brother. She's known since day one, a few months into working together, and she doesn't judge. One more reason I love her.

She finally answers my question regarding whether or not she's getting laid. "Unfortunately no, not since the Rivera Maya."

My brow lifts at the memory of sunshine and mojitos on the white-sandy beaches. "That was a good trip." Another trip I met up with Nick on. *Damn, I can't get him off my mind.*

"Mmm hmmm," Autumn hums and reaches into the mini bar, grabbing a bottle of water for herself before sitting cross legged on the end of the bed.

"I have no idea why you don't snag someone and settle down," I comment after plugging in my charger and then fishing out my phone from my bag to plug in while we're up here. I already have a dozen emails and four messages waiting for me. And wait they will continue to do. After the flight I had today, everything can wait until tomorrow morning. The conference doesn't start until noon and regardless of how late we stay out tonight; I'll be up at six. It's something about these events, maybe the excitement or the social interaction… whatever it is, I can never sleep. It doesn't matter how comfy the mattress is or how plush the pure white comforters are. Unless Nick happens to wear me out in bed. My thighs involuntarily clench at the thought. I check the messages just to be sure. None are from Nick and my heart drops a little.

Autumn holds up her finger, closing her eyes for a moment of silence so she can yawn again and oblige, and then dig into the bottom of my now nearly empty bag for the foldable steamer and set it on the floor of the closet, next to a set of sexy black heels, although they're simple the heels are so thin, they reek of sex appeal.

I make sure my heels are hot, my lingerie a class-A knockout and my dress, professional and nothing less. Simple and natural makeup, but a bold red lip. I love confidence and I wear it subtly, but to pack a punch. It may seem like an oxymoron, but it works for me. It keeps me lifted and motivated. So long as I have sexy panties and a pedicure, I'm convinced I can conquer the world.

It takes me a minute of digging at the bottom of my nearly empty bag for the extra charger for my laptop before I realize Autumn isn't talking anymore. Lifting my gaze, I see her fiddling on her phone.

"Hey, I thought you said something about 'getting some'?" I remind her.

She smiles brightly at me even though sleep is written all over her expression, holding up her phone and says simply, "Your star crossed lover is here."

## OLIVIA

*T*he bar is slightly darker than everywhere else on the main level of the hotel. The lights are softer. So dim that the lit glass shelves lined with glass bottles behind the bar are really the main attraction. Although it's a Friday night, it's nearly midnight and most of the guests on this level are gathered around a stone fireplace, leaving the bar stools vacant and perfect for a private conversation. There's only a single couple seated at the bar and then there's me and my red dress.

My heart's been racing ever since I left Autumn in our hotel room to come down here. I don't remember being this eager before. I don't remember missing him as much as I am right now. "What'll it be?" the bartender asks me. Resting her palms on the

13

bar, she leans forward to tell me when I purse my lips in indecision, "The cosmos here are pretty stellar." Her perfectly pluck brow raises as if to ask, *want one?*

"I'll have one of those then," I answer with a smile that's relatively genuine. All the nerves have me on edge. With a pat on the bar and a "coming right up," the bartender turns her back to me to make a pretty concoction of liquor in a tall skinny glass. I can't help it even though I'm irritated with my own impatience; I peek at the clock on the wall at the far end. It's only been ten minutes of waiting. It's still ten minutes too long for my taste.

With a tap on my phone, I bring up the text messages. *Meet you at the bar.* He texted it nearly fifteen minutes ago. Not even a half minute after Autumn telling me her brother was here, he texted me. And that's all he said: *Meet you at the bar.*

He gave the command and I obliged.

I don't remember being this needy ever before. But then again, I can't remember ever waiting on him. This time feels different. And I don't like it.

"Here you are," the bartender's voice is soft like the smile on her lips. Thanking her and then taking a sip, I pretend like I don't want to text him. I've never been *that* girl. Clingy, and left wanting. I've been busy all my life and for the last few years, Nicholas has been right there every step of the way, never making me feel like things weren't enough.

I just want him here. The second he's here, I know everything will be alright and this weird anxiousness will be gone.

"Did you wear red for me?" The seductive cadence and deep voice behind me eases everything in me in an instant. From my head to my toes, including those butterflies in the pit of my stomach. I don't have time to turn around, his strong arms wrap around my front, his shoulders cradling me as Nick kisses my neck. Right there, in that spot just beneath my ear that's so sensitive. His rough stubble tickles my neck as he leaves me. It leaves me hot and bothered, but so relaxed. So very at home. That's how it feels with him. He feels like home even though I never see him there. It's always hotels. Still, that doesn't change how I feel.

I reach up and behind me, my fingers trailing along his short hair until he brings his lips to meet mine. Pressing them lightly at first, until my lips mold to his. I part mine for him, and he nips slightly before deepening the kiss.

Even when he kisses me, the smile doesn't leave. It never falters. The electric tingle races through me, from head to toe. Until he breaks the kisses, leaving me breathless and trailing the tip of his nose against mine.

"So did you?" he asks, taking the seat next to me and I'm in such a haze, I don't remember why he's waiting for an answer. His handsome smirk widens into a grin when he sees the effect he has on me. "Wear the red dress for me?"

"Oh," the blush rises to my cheeks before I answer, "You know I did." I haven't an ounce of game in me. That's what Autumn says and she's right. I don't care to either. I'm not here for games.

"I love it," he comments and before I can let my smitten comeback get the better of me, the bartender's back.

"Hello, there. What'll it be?" she asks Nicholas and takes a glance at my glass, still nearly full as Nick looks at what's on tap.

He's going to get the lager. I know it. He knows it. But he takes his time, looking at each one before telling her, "A lager please."

"Short or..."

"Tall," he's quick to answer.

"Tough day?" I tease him as he slips off his jacket and gets comfortable, adjusting on the stool.

"Long," he answers and slips his hand over

mine. The tips of his fingers toy with mine. "It's got a good ending though." He smirks, before lifting my hand to his lips, kissing my knuckles one at a time.

"Hasn't anyone told you, flattery will get you everywhere," I joke and he laughs. A deep rough sound that I love.

"Maybe once or twice," he answers and thanks the bartender as she places his beer in front of him.

He doesn't waste any time, taking a long swig although his left hand stays over mine. He doesn't look at me after and suddenly the air feels different again. That instinctive flip in my stomach goes off and I pull my hand away to readjust in my seat.

"You doing okay?" I ask him. My nerves get the better of me. I always trust my gut, I have all my life and it's never steered me wrong. If things feel off, it's because they are off.

He hesitates before letting out a small huff that's a humorless laugh and running his hand up the back of his neck.

"I might be moving soon," he tells me and wraps both of his hands around his beer.

Flip, skitter, halt. That's what my heart does.

"Oh yeah," I suck at keeping the nerves out of my voice. "Where to?" I ask him because it's the polite thing to do. It's the obvious question. Even though nerves dance along my heated skin.

"Out of state, the company is still nailing down the details," he answers me and I watch the cords in his neck tighten as he swallows.

"Oh, when will you know?" Anticipation and slight relief are there, but still, this is a serious conversation. And we don't have those. Not about us. If ever one of us needs something, we're there for each other, but those moments are few and far between. I don't recall a single conversation we've ever had about "us." Although I'm completely aware, that's exactly what this is.

"This week."

"Really?" My brow shoots up my face and I can't stop it. It gets a huff of laughter from Nick, who nods his head and takes another gulp of his beer. "Really," he answers. "What do you think about that?"

"About you no longer being available for our get togethers on a whim?" I clarify, merely to take up time so I can find the right answer.

"Yeah," his voice is low, coaxing. "Will you miss me?"

There's a pitter patter in my chest that lights up

every nerve ending in me. "Of course I will," I answer honestly.

"Yeah," he agrees, "I don't know for sure yet." The thick air around us dissipates into a casualness that's familiar.

"Company decision?" I question and he nods.

"Yeah, something like that," he teases and absently runs his thumb along the dew of his beer glass.

"It's weighing on you?" I question, noting how he seems lost in the conflict of whether or not to move.

"It's a big decision," he says but the way he says it sounds as if it's not so unordinary.

"So if you moved… we wouldn't be able to meet up in hotels anymore. And have our dirty little secret rendezvous."

"Is that what this is? I'm your dirty little secret?" he toys with me and I gently smack his arm and then return to nursing my drink.

"Seriously though, is that why this feels different?" I almost ask, why it feels like all of this is a long goodbye, but I don't.

"Things just… they might change a little and I wasn't sure what you'd think about it," he tells me and a nervousness settles in my gut. Change. Sometimes when I use that word, my clients get this wide-eyed, defensive look. I can feel it coming over me.

"We don't need to talk about it," I'm quick to shut it down. "All I want tonight is a kiss. Is that too much for a girl to ask?" I don't want to talk about this right now. There are too many unknowns and what ifs and I am not ready to say goodbye when he's just sat down. I know that's where this is headed and I'm not ready. I'm not willing to agree to goodbye. Or to going back to being friends. That's exactly what this feels like.

"Mmm," Nick hums and then leans close to me, kissing me and silencing my inward complaints. The kiss isn't deep, but it's soothing and when he breaks it, I keep my eyes closed for just a moment longer, wanting to make sure I remember it forever.

I whisper with my eyes still closed, "God, I missed you."

## NICHOLAS

*H*er long blonde hair is a messy halo from her running her fingers through her locks. It only adds to the sex kitten look she has going on. I love that she did it for me, even more that she's not ashamed to admit it out loud.

If only I wasn't afraid of losing this, these moments of inhibition with this captivating woman, I'd tell her right now what's happening. I'd tell her everything's changed and lay it out for her to accept or to walk away.

"Your room?" she asks, her eyes half lidded as she bites down into her bottom lip.

"Damn right," I answer her beneath my breath, leaving cash on the bar and then helping her off her stool. Her small hand slips into mine and I lead her towards the elevators, listening to click of her heels and loving how she holds on to our clasped hands with her other, her shoulder brushing against mine as we walk, as if she needs to touch me, needs to have her body close to mine.

I get it. I more than get it. I love it. Which is why I'm not ready for change, but something had to give. I live for these moments with her, after tonight, it'll never be the same again.

"You smell like man," Olivia hums when the elevator dings and the doors slide open.

"Is that right?" I question, hitting the button for my floor and waiting for the doors to close as my cock hardens to an unbearable degree.

There's a hair of an opening, before they shut completely, and I lift her hands above her head, gripping her wrists and pushing her small body against the elevator wall with mine. It's quick, it's instinctual. A simmering want and desire rushes through me, when she gasps and I catch it, sealing my mouth over hers with a kiss.

"Nick," she moans in my mouth and I love it. She rocks her body against my length and my response is a deep groan of need that vibrates through my chest.

Nipping her bottom lip, I release her the second I feel the elevator slow. I only have a moment to adjust my cock in my pants and stare down at her breathless, sagging against the wall.

"Two more minutes," I tell her, hoping to ease the ache so obvious on her face. With my hand out, she takes it, righting herself and the doors open. No one's here to watch us, no one in the hall, but still, we're professional. Her clients could be on this floor after all, and she prefers discretion, apart from a kiss here and there.

I can't count the number of times I've slipped a key card into the door with Olivia behind me, caressing my arm and waiting patiently for the soft beep and gentle click of the door being opened. It's a heady rush each and every time. The anticipation, the desire that flows freely between us. From the first time, a drunken night with a goodnight kiss turned into more, to two weeks ago, it only gets better with Olivia.

She leaves me wanting more.

Pushing the door open, I motion for her to enter first, and whether she's tipsy from the wine or drunk on lust, Olivia slides past me, making sure her curves brush against me as she does.

Her hips sway and the simmer in my blood only gets hotter.

The door closes with a resounding click and I

don't have to command her, she turns at the foot of the bed, facing me as she unzips her dress and lets it fall from the curve of her shoulders down to a puddle of fine fabric at her feet. She makes a move to take her heels off next and I stop her.

"No," I order, "keep them on tonight." My voice is deep and I let her hear every ounce of need I have for her. Her lips part just slightly, her breasts rising with the quick inhale in the quiet room, and I swear my cock leaks precum at the sight of her, turned on by the simple fact that I'll fuck her tonight in those sex kitten heels.

I could imagine her lying on the bed behind her, her legs in the air as I pound into her, then the slim heels dragging down my back as she screams my name. I could, but I don't, because her hazel eyes entrance me, reflecting the same concoction of need and want in the moonlit room. The thick curtains are open, but the sheer ones are closed, giving a breathtaking view.

The mountain range behind her, the bright moon that filters into the room against the plush white comforter. And in front of it all, a beautiful woman who wants me as badly as I want her, slowly but surely, unstrapping her bra and letting it fall to the floor.

With her fingers moving to her hips, I motion for her to stop and finally move, closing the distance between us in three long strides. Every step closer, the collar around my neck feels tighter, suffocating me for still being dressed.

She tilts her head for me to kiss her, but I don't. Her eyes are closed and it takes a moment before she opens them, staring up at me as I tower over her naked form, all but heels and thin satin panties. "Hands at your sides," I tell her and she listens. She loves the submission as much as I love the domination. She knows it all now, every command, every wish I have. "Fucking perfect," I mutter beneath my breath, letting her see my gaze roam down her body.

Trailing my thumb down her bottom lip, I let it fall to her collarbone, then lower, teasing her breasts one at a time. It's the only touch I give her for now. Her soft moan fills the room and her eyes close as her head falls back, lost in pleasure.

I take my time, still fully clothed, dragging my touch down her body to rid her of the red thong. She only touches me when I bend down, her hand on my shoulder, to step out of the underwear.

Tossing it carelessly beside us, I keep my gaze on her, and plant a kiss just beneath her navel, then lower, dragging the tip of my nose down further until I'm right where I want to be, my lips at her clit. I suckle gently and her fingertips brush my shoulders, but she's quick to correct herself.

"Nick," my name is a mix of a pant and a moan on her lips. I taste her, parting her lips and dipping two thick fingers inside her. She's already wet, already whimpering. I stroke her, curling my fingers to be sure to hit the sweet spot at her front wall.

"Please," she begs with true desperation as she sways, without anything to keep her steady but the heels she chose to wear tonight. Her arousal coats my fingers as I stroke more ruthlessly, pulling her pleasure from her. Her smell, her soft sounds and even the heat of her body being so close is addictive. She's a drug and I've been addicted for as long as I can remember.

I can barely take it, crouched down in front of her, hard with my own need and desperate to be inside her. Quickening my movements, I suck on her clit and the instant gasp is followed by her nails digging into my shoulders as she clenches around my fingers and screams out my name.

I withdraw in an instant, all too aware that she's already gone over the edge, finding her orgasm.

*Smack*! My hand lands hard on her ass in reprimand and she can't even jump, her balance is so disturbed from her pleasure that she falls into me. "Bad girl," I growl at her ear as I lift her by her ass, throwing her onto the bed behind her.

I don't waste the moment undressing. In an instant I'm between her legs, still clothed and nipping her neck. My right hand travels up her body, my left unzips my pants and pulls out my cock. I stroke it once, before slamming into her.

She screams out, her neck arching, her mouth the perfect "o" and I stay just like that, buried to the hilt for only a moment. Just one to let her adjust. That's when I finally kiss her, my tongue delving into her hot mouth and silencing her strangled screams of pleasure as I ravage her.

Pistoning my hips, gripping her own to keep her where I want her. Her heels thud as they hit the floor, one by one, unable to stay on as I fuck her ruthlessly.

She's so tight, so hot and so close to coming again already. Her second release is what pushes me to have mine.

I groan her name in the crook of her neck, feeling the warm air of her moans on my cheek as she cums with me. Pulsing around me as the waves of my own release pulse through me.

Both of us breathless, both of us sated, I slip out

slowly watching her wince as I do. She rolls on her side, breathing heavily with her eyes closed.

I pull the covers around her before heading to the bathroom, finally stripping down and gathering a warm washcloth to take care of her.

It's silent until I climb in bed with her, everything taken care of so she can fall asleep. "Sleep well," I tell her, knowing she'll stay with me tonight

She doesn't though and I'm certain I can't either.

*This could be our last time together.* There's no way I could possibly sleep. Her fingers trail along the grooves in my chest, and when she brings them up higher I lean down to kiss her hand.

She hums in satisfaction, but she still doesn't sleep. I could bore her to sleep, talking about the merger that just went through and how the company is sky rocketing, the stocks booming. She'd listen to it all, with the same expression she gives me now, as if I'm her beloved Prince Charming.

"I don't want to sleep," she finally breaks the silence.

"What do you want for Christmas, Olivia?" I ask her, running my thumb down the curve of her neck and feeling the pull of my lips into a smirk when she shivers.

Naked and tired, Olivia stretches lazily and then

sidles up closer to me under the sheets, "More of this," she answers and I have to keep my expression the same, unmoving, so she doesn't see the loss I feel deep inside. Her eyes are closed, but I don't want to risk her seeing.

"Nothing else?" I question, knowing she isn't going to get more of these meet ups. Not for a while at least with all of the changes coming.

Slowly peeking up at me, her hazel eyes a mix of wildfire and calming ocean shores, "Fine, all I want is a kiss." Her voice is soft and her hand on my chest even softer. Leaning down to kiss her, I let the kiss linger, waiting for her to hum in approval. She does and I knew she would. I love that sound. I love how easily she kisses me.

"I hate that I have to leave you tomorrow," she says it so easily, so used to it. She's alright with what we have. She would be fine with this for as long as I let it happen.

"Hopefully I'll see you soon," I answer her and her eyes open, staring at my chest rather than meeting my gaze.

"Do you know when that will be?" she questions.

I hate that I have to answer her the way I do, "No," I tell her.

I bet she thinks she's gotten away with hiding her

disappointment, but I see it. "That's alright," she tells me, even though I know she feels that same ache in her chest I do at the thought of not having another night like this planned. She can't say goodbye so easily.

Her pointer traces my collarbone when she whispers what we've told each other every time for years now, "It's never goodbye. Only until next time."

OLIVIA

"*W*hy do I choose the walk of shame?"

Nick's first response to my groggy morning question is a rough chuckle that jostles the bed. "I can go get your things," he offers, "Or Autumn can bring them?"

I shake my head, brushing my cheek against his firm chest before resting my head back against him, "It's okay, I'll walk it with pride," I answer with a simper and lightheartedness.

The early morning sun is peeking in and I check the clock to find it's nearly eight. Last night filters in as my eyes adjust to morning and the easy rest in Nick's bed changes into the reality that I need to leave it and I may never share one with him again.

"You're really leaving?" I question but I didn't mean to. The disbelief simply slipped out.

He breathes in deep and his chest moves with it, so I remove myself from the cozy spot and sit up, covering myself with the sheets. As I do, the ache between my thighs intensifies. I'll feel him for days.

"Yeah, just one night this time. I have to get somethings settled," Nick doesn't look at me as he talks, instead he reaches for the bottle of water on the nightstand and hands it to me.

"Thanks," I tell him and my smile is weak. I drink down as many gulps as I can, trying to pause the unwanted thoughts filtering through my mind.

"You okay?"

"Huh?" I look up into Nick's steely blues to find them riddled with concern. "Fine," I lie. "I just have to get going."

With the excuse spilled, I gather the sheets, pushing them out of the way and search for my dress and underwear.

"You don't have to go. We can order in breakfast," he offers but there's no hope in his voice.

I was already a drink down last night, but still. How did I go to bed with him one last time, knowing that he was leaving? How did I think I could do it? Stay here with him and say goodbye?

I struggle with my strap and Nick climbs out of bed, still naked and in all his glory to help me.

"Olivia," his voice is gentle. "You don't have to run off," he whispers at my neck and then pulls my back into his chest.

"I'm not running off," I lie. "I just need a shower and to prepare."

I turn around, conscious of the fact that I haven't brushed my teeth. I usually use his toothbrush, but I also typically stay. This morning isn't typical. I can feel that in my bones.

"Never goodbye. Only until next time." He smiles when he says it and that's why I can only nod, not trusting myself to speak. With a wave of my hand, I leave him there, and put on a brave face when I open the door to my shared room with Autumn. I don't want her to know how much I'm breaking right now. Nothing is certain. He may not move. It may not be over. That thought is the only thing that keeps me glued together.

I wish next time was a given. For the first time since we started it, I'm all too aware that it's not a given. No matter how much I want to lie to myself.

THE TAXI RIDE is almost forty minutes long and it's excruciating. All I want is my pillow so I can bury my head in it and let all of these unwanted emotions out.

"I miss you already," the second the plane landed, I messaged Nick first. I haven't heard from him since we said goodbye at the resort and again, I find myself not used to the waiting. The lack of an answer from him. I check it again, and a good thirty minutes later, I have nothing. No answer from him.

I have loved every conference we've ever done, but not this one. This one is stained with loss. Undeniable and irrefutable loss. I glance at my phone again, to see no response from Nick. With tears pricking at the back of my eyes, I'm tempted to message Autumn. She's his sister and he's leaving me. Tension works its way into my gut and I shift on the leather backseats of the cab. They protest in response.

Is this really the end of it? It can't be. There's a sinking feeling in my chest and I need to talk to someone about it, but who? Autumn's the only one who knows, and what am I supposed to say to her? *Your brother is ignoring me?* We're grown adults and I knew what this was. I just wasn't prepared for this. We're never ready for goodbyes. At least I'm not. I thought I could avoid it with Nick, I thought I'd never have to say it. Checking my phone again and noting the lack of a message from him, I was apparently wrong. The conclusion I've come to is the worst of them all, because that's what my gut is telling me. *It's over.* He's moving on and that's all there is to it.

I keep thinking, it was too good to last. Wasn't it? It was so easy and natural. Everything always fell into place with Nick... I should have known better than to think it would last or become anything more. Fuck, it hurts. It's not supposed to hurt, when you keep yourself at a distance and make sure the relationship is casual. It's not supposed to hurt when it ends. But I'll be damned if that's not exactly what I'm feeling right now.

I check my phone and again, there's no response.

"Right up here," the taxi driver says absently and before I can answer, the words catch themselves at the back of my throat.

Oh my God, he's here.

My heart does that fluttering thing my stomach was doing only days ago. Sitting on the footsteps to my front porch, his large frame taking up the small threshold. I can't think straight, let alone breathe. He's right here. Waiting for me.

Nick must feel my eyes on him as the taxi slows in front of my townhouse because he looks right up at me. Those steely blues stealing my breath with their intensity.

My heart races, beating wildly at the sight of him.

"Mam?" the cab driver's voice alerts me that I need to pay and get on my way.

"Sorry, sorry," I answer breathlessly, frantically searching for cash so I can get out and go to the man I haven't been able to stop thinking about.

I don't have a chance to get my luggage, Nicholas gets it for me. Carrying it up to my porch steps and waiting there for me.

Anxiousness tingles its way through me and I barely hear the taxi drive off as I stand on the steps, looking up at him and whispering, "What are you doing here?" Praying and hoping he's here for more than a real goodbye.

## NICHOLAS

*What am I doing here?*

"Right now, I'm trying to gather up the strength to ask you something," I answer her. I can barely swallow, barely breathe. Even though it's winter and the cold is blistering, making the tip of Olivia's nose a rosy red already, I'm burning hot.

"I have to know, do you want me, Olivia? Do you want more?" Her bottom lip falls open and her hazel eyes widen with surprise. I can't bare for her to answer me without telling her everything, without giving this the best shot I can give it.

"Because I want you. I want all of you. I love our stolen nights and I'll do everything I can to keep giving them to you, but I need more." A quick intake and a single step forward, closing the distance between us is all that pauses the confession I've been working over in my head all week. "I want to be with you, really be with you. Every day and always. Not just a secret rendezvous. I want it all. The picket fence, kids, I want it all… with you. And only you."

I don't know if I've said it all and I'm certain I've said most of it wrong. I'm nervous and I'm terrified. Terrified that she doesn't want this. It will destroy me if she says no. She's all I want and all I've wanted since I first laid eyes on her.

She still hasn't said anything, although she takes a hesitant step forward and I use that closeness to take her hands in mine, running soothing circles along her wrists with the rough pad of my thumb.

"Do you want me, Olivia? Because I'll move here, with you or get my own place, so we can be together like we should. If you don't, I understand, but I need to know."

The silence is awful. It rips at me from the inside as I wait for her to say something. Every deep breath she takes I prepare for her to tell me no.

"You asked me what I want for Christmas. At the hotel, you asked me and I lied to you," her voice is soft and riddled with emotion but I can't decipher it. I need an answer.

"I know. A kiss. You said all you wanted was a

kiss." I can't bear it if she tells me that now. I'm not ready to say goodbye. I nearly backtrack, I nearly give in and tell her I'll go back to only hotel rooms and discreet rendezvous if that's what she wants.

"I lied. I lied to you," her voice cracks and it echoes the feeling in my heart. "I want so much more than a kiss. All I want for Christmas, is you."

Relief washes over me and it comes with a warmth I'm unfamiliar with. It's better than the heat between us when I first see her across the bar. It feels like home.

"I couldn't tell you because A, it's cheesy and B, I didn't think I could have you."

"Just say the word, and I'll move here. I'm ready to be with you, Olivia, I don't think I can fathom not being able to see you again."

"Same," she breathes the single word.

"That's a yes? You want this? You want me?"

"All of you." She nods, quickly and vigorously. Tears make her hazel eyes glassy. "I want all of you too."

*Thank fuck.*

I can't describe the relief, immediate and all consuming. With one arm scooping around the small of her back and the other spearing into her

39

hair, I kiss her, the woman I love, with everything I have.

"I love you, Olivia," I tell her for the first time, solidifying what we have. What we've had all this time but neither of us was willing to risk bringing it to life.

"I love you too," she whispers against my lips, in the warm air between us. "You don't have to leave do you?"

"I took two weeks off to figure all this out. I want to figure it out with you. I told Autumn. She knows."

"She does?" her eyes are full of shock. It's comical really.

"You can't be mad; I swore her to secrecy." There's a smirk on my lips and before she can answer, I kiss her again. And again.

She nuzzles her nose against mine, before looking up through her thick lashes. "Two weeks to figure it all out?"

"Yeah, and if we need more time, I'll make it. I want us. More than anything, I know I need you."

"I figured it out. Move in with me and let's spend two weeks in bed." She says it so seriously, yet easily. As if it's so simple and I chuckle, planting a kiss on her forehead that makes her smile. She has the most beautiful smile.

"We can start with me helping take your luggage inside," I offer and she nods watching me while I gather her things and she opens the door. The moment it closes, she's on me, her arms wrapping around me with a fierceness. Dropping the bags to the floor, I hold her back.

"I thought... I thought we weren't going to get this," she whispers and before I can ask what she means, she kisses me, standing in my arms on her tip toes. "You make me happy and I don't want to be without you." She speaks so quietly, I barely hear her.

"Same," I tell her, brushing her hair back and waiting for her to finally look up at me.

"I've never been the girl for fairytales, but I want a happily ever after with you."

Resting my forehead against hers, all I can focus on is the warmth in my chest. Everything about this, about *her*, feels right.

"You can say it again," she tells me. "Tell me you love me again."

"I love you Olivia. I want to love you forever."

"I love you too."

**Merciless World**

A Kiss to Tell

Possessive

Merciless
Heartless
Breathless
Endless

All He'll Ever Be

A Kiss To Keep

A Single Glance
A Single Kiss
A Single Touch

Hard to Love
Desperate to Touch
Tempted to Kiss
Easy to Fall

**Merciless World Spin Off**

It's Our Secret

**Standalone Novels:**
Broken
Forget Me Not

**Sins and Secrets Duets:**
Imperfect (Imperfect Duet book 1)
Unforgiven (Imperfect Duet book 2)

Damaged (Damaged Duet book 1)
Scarred (Damaged Duet book 2)

**Willow Winters**
**Standalone Novels:**

Tell Me To Stay
Second Chance
Knocking Boots
Promise Me
Burned Promises

**Collections**
Don't Let Go
Deepen The Kiss

**Valetti Crime Family Series:**
Dirty Dom
His Hostage
Rough Touch
Cuffed Kiss
Bad Boy

**Highest Bidder Series,
cowritten with Lauren Landish:**
Bought
Sold
Owned
Given

**Bad Boy Standalones,
cowritten with Lauren Landish:**

Inked

Tempted

Mr. CEO


Forsaken, cowritten with B. B. Hamel


Happy reading and best wishes,


W Winters xx

## ABOUT THE AUTHOR

Thank you so much for reading my romances. I'm just a stay at home mom and avid reader turned author and I couldn't be happier.
I hope you love my books as much as I do!

More by Willow Winters
www.willowwinterswrites.com/books/

Made in the USA
Middletown, DE
30 September 2023

39703194R00031